P9-DTU-413

*Other Books by Mitsumasa Anno*
*published by Philomel Books*

Anno's Animals

Anno's Britain

Anno's Counting House

Anno's Flea Market

Anno's Italy

Anno's Journey

Anno's Magical ABC:
An Anamorphic Alphabet

Anno's Mysterious Multiplying Jar

Anno's U.S.A.

The King's Flower

The Unique World of Mitsumasa Anno:
Selected Works (1969–1977)

The publishers gratefully acknowledge the assistance of
Mr. Frederic Tudor in the translation of the text for this book.

First U.S.A. edition 1985. Published by Philomel Books, a member of The Putnam Publishing Group, 51 Madison Avenue, New York, N.Y. 10010.  Printed in Japan.

Library of Congress Cataloging in Publication Data. Nozaki, Akihiro, Anno's hat tricks. Translation of: Akai bōshi. Summary: Three children, Tom, Hannah, and Shadowchild, who represents the reader, are made to guess, using the concept of binary logic, the color of the hats on their heads. An introduction to logical thinking and mathematical problem-solving. 1. Problem solving—Juvenile literature. 2. Logic—Juvenile literature. 3. Binary system (Mathematics)—Juvenile literature. [1. Problem solving. 2. Logic. 3. Binary system (Mathematics) 4. Mathematics] I. Anno, Mitsumasa . II. Title. QA63.A5613 1985 153.4′3 84-18900

ISBN 0-399-21212-4

# ANNO'S HAT TRICKS

Text by Akihiro Nozaki

Pictures by Mitsumasa Anno

PHILOMEL BOOKS

*New York*

Hello! I'm a hatter. I have lots of hats in my box.
Let me show you some tricks you can play with them.

This is the shadow of a child. Please think of it as your own shadow. In this book, I will call you Shadowchild.

Here are Tom and Hannah.
They are good friends of yours.

If they will please shut their eyes for a moment,
I'll put hats on their heads.

Please shut your eyes too, Shadowchild, and then turn the page.
After you have turned the page, you may open your eyes.

I put a hat on Tom and one on you, Shadowchild.
Shadowchild, can you tell me the color of Tom's hat?
"It's red."
Yes, it's red.

What color is *your* hat, Shadowchild?
Is it red? Or is it white?
(It looks like black to you because all you can see
is its shadow. It could be red or white.)

The correct answer is "I don't know."
You can see other people's hats, but you can't see your own.
Now, please close your eyes again, and turn the page.

I'll take one red hat and one white hat,
and put one on Tom and one on you, Shadowchild.
Now you may open your eyes.

Tom, can you tell me the color of your hat?
"Yes, it's red."
That's right, but how did you know?
"Well, really, I just guessed it."
Oh! But you can tell for sure, if you think about it a bit.

Now, Shadowchild, can you tell me the
color of your hat? (Shadowchild is you, the reader,
so you should try to figure out the answer here.)

There are two hats; one is red and one is white.
Since Tom's hat is red, Shadowchild, then your hat must be white.

The next trick is a little harder. I'll take two red hats and one white hat. I'll put one on Tom and one on Shadowchild.

Shadowchild, can you tell me the color of your hat? "No, I can't."

Very good. Of course you can't.
Since Tom's hat is red, one more red hat and one white hat remain. You can't tell which one is on your head.

Once more, I'll take two red hats and one white hat;
and I'll put one on Tom and one on you, Shadowchild.
This time, I'll ask Tom first.

Tom, what color is your hat?
"It's red. This time, I'm sure about it."
Good.

Now, Shadowchild, can you tell me the color of your hat?
"No, I can't."

No? That's strange. You should be able to. Think a little more.
Why could Tom be sure about *his* hat's color?
Think about the reason, and turn the page.

How could Tom tell the color of his hat
without seeing it?
He can see *your* hat, Shadowchild.

If your hat is white, then Tom will think:
  "Shadowchild's hat is white.
  There is only one white hat.
  So, mine is red."

That's easy.
But if your hat is red, then Tom will think this way:
  "Shadowchild's hat is red.
  There are two red hats.
  So, I can't tell whether mine is red or white."

Tom says he is sure his hat is red.

Now then, what color is *your* hat, Shadowchild?

Let's see now.

If Shadowchild's hat is white,
then Tom can tell that his own hat is red.
If Shadowchild's hat is red,
then Tom won't be able to tell the color of his hat.

Since Tom answered clearly that his was red,
then your hat must be white, Shadowchild.

At first you had no way of telling. But then, after hearing Tom's answer, you could tell your hat's color correctly.

Here's another tricky question. I'll take two red
hats and one white hat; and put one of them on
Tom and one on you, Shadowchild. These may be two
red hats, or a red hat and a white one.
I won't tell you which.

I'll ask Tom first.
What is the color of your hat, Tom?
"I don't know."
Now, Shadowchild, what is the color of *your* hat?

"Red."
Are you sure?
"Yes, it's red."
But can you explain why it must be red?

If your hat is white, then Tom should have said
"Mine is red!"
But he said "I don't know." So *your* hat must be red.

Isn't it interesting? Tom's answer, "I don't know," gives you the clue to the color of your own hat.

Now let's play a trick with three children: Tom, Hannah, and you, Shadowchild.
I'll take two red hats and one white hat, and put one on each child. Hannah, what color is your hat?
"It's white."
Good. Tom, what color is yours?
"White."
White? Why?
"Oh, I made a mistake. You took two red hats, so mine must be red."
Now, Shadowchild, what color is your hat?
"It's red."
Yes, that's right. I used one white hat and two red hats.

Now, please shut your eyes, and I'll rearrange the hats.

I have rearranged the hats.
Shadowchild, what color is your hat?
"It's white."
Very good!

Now let's try a harder trick.
Please shut your eyes, and turn the page.

This time I'll take three red hats and two white hats,
and I'll put one on each of the three children.
So, they may have three red hats, or two red hats
and one white hat, or a red hat and two white hats.
But they can't all wear white hats.
Shadowchild, can you tell me the color of your hat?
"No, I can't."

Good! Of course you can't.
Let's try again. I'll rearrange the hats.

Shadowchild, what color is your hat?
"It's red."
Good! There are only two white hats.
Somebody will have a red one.
So if two children have white hats,
then yours must be red.

Now, Tom, can you tell me the color of your hat?
"No, I can't."
Think! —Shadowchild could tell me the color of his hat.
"Ah, then mine is white."

Very good! If the first person said “Mine is red,”
then the others must have white hats.

I'll take three red hats and two white hats and put one on each of the three children. At least one person will have a red hat.

I'll ask Hannah first.
Hannah, what color is your hat?
"It's red."
Good!

Now, Shadowchild, what color is yours?
"White."

Very good! But can you explain why yours must be white?

If both Tom and you, Shadowchild, have white hats,
then Hannah can say "Mine is red," since I said
there must be at least one person wearing a red hat.
But if either Tom or Shadowchild has a red one,
then Hannah's hat could be either red or white.
She wouldn't be able to tell for sure. But she answered
clearly, "It's red." So both Tom and Shadowchild
must have on white hats.

Once again, the other person's answer helped you to answer.

Again, I'll take three red hats and two white ones, and put one on each of the three children. This way you know that at least one child will have a red hat.

I'll ask Tom first.
Tom, what color is your hat?
"I don't know."
Now, Hannah, what color is yours?
"I don't know."
Well, then, Shadowchild, can you tell me the color of your hat?

You can, if you think about it.
If you can't get the answer, turn the page.

Both Tom and Hannah have on red hats, so you don't know whether yours is red or white.
But Tom said "I don't know."
Both you and Hannah heard him say it. It may help you get the answer, if you think it over.
If both you and Hannah had white hats, then Tom would have said "Mine is red." But he said "I don't know," so at least one of you must have a red hat.

After Tom said "I don't know," I asked the same question of Hannah, and she also said "I don't know."

What does it mean? Let's imagine what Hannah thought.

Hannah can't see her own hat, but she can see the other persons' hats, and she heard Tom's answer, so she knows that either she or Shadowchild must have a red hat. Perhaps if Shadowchild's hat were white, then she would know that her own was the red one, and she would have said "My hat is red." But if Shadowchild's hat is red, then Hannah can't tell for sure whether hers is red or white.

If Shadowchild's is white,
Hannah will know hers is red.
If Shadowchild's is red,
Hannah can't tell her hat's color.

Hannah thought about it carefully, and then said "I don't know." That means your hat must be red, Shadowchild!

Do you understand it, Shadowchild? If you really do, then turn the page. If you're still not sure, please go back to the beginning of the book and start reading again. If you truly want to understand these tricks, you need to read slowly and carefully.

The final trick is very hard. I'll take three red hats and two white hats, and put one on each of the three children.
At least one child will have a red hat.
I ask Tom first.
Tom, what color is your hat?
"I don't know."
Now, Hannah, what color is yours?
"It's red."
Finally, I ask you, Shadowchild.
What color is *your* hat?

This is a very hard question. If you can work the answer out by yourself, you're terrific! Please give it a try!

## *A Note to Parents and Other Older Readers*

The hatter in this book is really devoted to introducing readers to the magic word "if." All his tricks can be solved with this word. "If" is a very small word, but it is one of the most powerful ones in our language. It is the key to imaginative thinking, a key that opens the door to new ideas. Yet "if" can also be used very strictly, to test the truth of an idea or a supposition in a logical way. Computer programmers use this kind of logic in their calculations. So do mathematicians and other scientists. The pattern of reasoning that goes "if . . . , then . . ." is very useful. It is no exaggeration to say that modern mathematics has been developed by using the word "if."

But why is this word "if" so important? It is a tricky word; it can cause some meaningless confusions. For instance, there is a French proverb that says: "By using the little word 'if,' we can put all of Paris inside a bottle." This means that we can say that anything, no matter how strange it sounds, is possible under certain arbitrary conditions. So, if we could make a bottle big enough, then we could put all of Paris inside it. Yes, it could be true. But it is not a very good way to use this word. We should refrain from abusing this wonderful "if"—especially for making lame excuses!

However, the word "if" is the best device for seeing some kinds of reality. By considering how it might feel "if I were Mommy" or what one might do "if one were in the same situation as Alan," we can understand the feelings and actions of other people much better. In such cases, "if" can be the first step toward loving our neighbor.

The word "if" is important also in the literary world of fantasy. Children can easily identify themselves with characters in a story, and see everything through their eyes. It is much more difficult for us adults. But we can still think in an "if I were . . ." manner, and then we can find our way much more readily into the magic forest where enchanted creatures beckon to us.

The word "if" is very useful in the scientific world, too. When a man looks at an apple falling from a tree and wonders: "What if the moon and the stars are also attracted to the earth by the same force that pulls the apple down . . ." then he may discover the law of universal gravitation. Mathematicians see things especially deeply through the word "if."

The first ten pages of this book contain some very simple "tricks." These are just warming-up exercises. Some children may say these are too easy for them, but it is very important to understand them clearly before going on to the harder ones. So don't skip these pages; rather, read them carefully.

On page 14, you will meet the word "if" for the first time in this book. Let us look at this page.

Here is one assumption: "If Shadowchild's hat is white, then Tom can tell that his own hat is red." This assumption agrees with the fact that Tom said "Mine is red."

Here is the second assumption: "If Shadowchild's hat is red, then Tom won't be able to tell the color of his hat." This second assumption doesn't agree with what Tom said, so it doesn't fit the facts.

But we should be very careful in using this kind of reasoning. We have said something like this: "The first assumption, that Shadowchild's hat is white, agrees with the fact that Tom said 'Mine is red.' *Therefore* Shadowchild's hat *must be* white." It is true in this case that Shadowchild's hat *is* white.

But this kind of reasoning is not *always* valid. We cannot use the words "therefore" and "must" in all situations, even though the assumption fits *some* of the facts. We may need more information in order to eliminate other possibilities.

For instance, suppose that a friend says to you, "Hey, my pet laid some eggs for me this morning!" You may say, "Splendid! But I didn't know you had a pet. What kind of a pet do you have?"

"Ah, you must guess," says your friend.

Well, you think, is it a hen? Maybe. A hen could lay some eggs for him, so it agrees with what your friend said. The assumption fits the fact. But you cannot conclude that *therefore* it *must be* a hen. It could also be a goldfish, a frog, or even an alligator! All of these creatures lay eggs. There are many possibilities, each of which fits, so we still do not know what it really is.

Now, how about a cat? Oh, but this is impossible, since cats don't lay eggs. So his pet can't be a cat, a tiger, or a lion. It can't be a dog, either. We are sure about that, and we can eliminate such cases, which don't agree with the known facts.

In this book, we are solving the problem of the color of a hat in the same way, by using the process of elimination and binary logic. In the example on page 14, the assumption that Shadowchild's hat is red doesn't agree with what Tom said. Tom said his hat was red. There were only two possibilities. We have now eliminated one: Shadowchild's hat can't be red. Since the hat can be only red or white, we can then conclude that Shadowchild's hat is white. This is perfectly good reasoning, because in this case there are no other possibilities. This is a simple case of binary logic.

But on page 22, we consider a problem involving three children. This is a much more complicated problem. However, we can still solve it by the process of elimination and binary logic. This is the way mathematicians and computers solve even very difficult problems. Computers are programmed to find answers by making binary choices. If you think carefully, you can solve the problems in this book in your head. But sometimes it is helpful to draw a diagram, showing all the possibilities. Then you can cross out, or eliminate, all the situations that do not fit the facts, until you have only the correct answer left. This is what computers are programmed to do.

Let us take another problem with Tom, Hannah, and Shadowchild. Our hatter has three red hats and two white hats. He has put a hat on each child. Figure 1 shows all the possible arrangements of the hats.

Here are the possibilities.

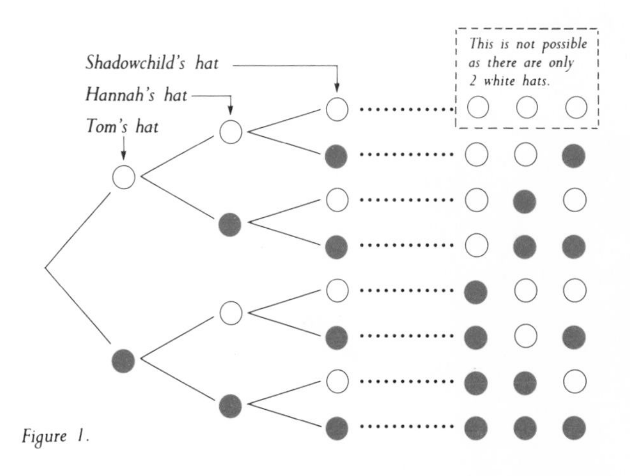


*Figure 1.*

Now the hatter asks Tom the color of his hat. If Tom says "Mine is red," then it's easy; the hats of the other two children must be white. But if Tom says "I don't know," then at least one of the other two children has a red hat. After this, setting aside the first child, the problem comes down to the two-person case we have already met with.

To eliminate the wrong answers and find the right one, we must use logic.

*Figure 2.*

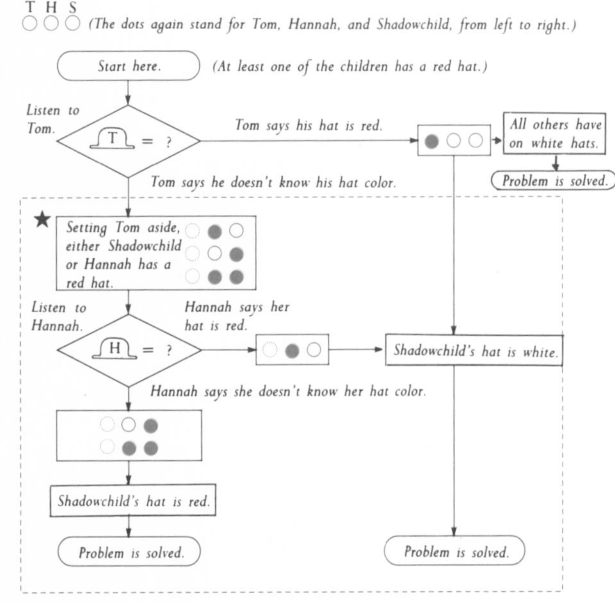


*(*The area enclosed by the dotted lines represents the two-person case of Hannah and Shadowchild.)*

If you understand this point, then you can solve the same problem for any number of children: four, seven, or even a hundred. As long as the number of white hats available is one less than the number of children, at least one of the children will always be wearing a red hat. Let's see how it goes for four children. If one of the four says "I don't know what color my hat is," then at least one of the other three children is wearing a red hat. Now you repeat the same question to another one of them. If the second child also says "I don't know the color of my hat," then at least one of the remaining two children has a red hat. If a child says "My hat is red," then the hats of the remaining children, who have not yet been asked, are all white. Thus the last child can always tell the color of his or her own hat.

This is not an easy puzzle, but if you are a puzzle-lover like our hatter, then please consider the case of five children who are given hats, at least one of which is red, and the rest of which may be red or white. Have a good time!

A.N.

---

AKIHIRO NOZAKI is a well-known writer of many popular books in his native Japan, including *The Sophistry, The Theory of Paradoxes, The Book of Solitaires,* and *The Story of Pi.* Born in Yokohama, in Kanezawa prefecture, in 1936, he studied mathematics at Tokyo University (Todai) and has since taught both mathematics and computer science at several universities in Japan. He is now Professor and Head of the Mathematics Department at International Christian University. Dr. Nozaki's interest in mathematics combines well with his fascination with fantasy, science fiction and the world of games.

MITSUMASA ANNO is famous for his many highly original and thought-provoking picture books, in recognition of which he was awarded the Hans Christian Andersen Medal, the highest honor given in the field of children's books. Born in Tsuwano in 1926, he studied at the Yamaguchi Teacher Training College. He taught at an independent school for several years before he decided to devote himself entirely to painting and writing. His home is now in a suburb of Tokyo, but he travels all over the world to do research for his many books. Mr. Anno feels that the mathematical laws that underlie nature are as beautiful as other aspects of the wonderful world we live in, and that even very young children can understand and appreciate them if they are clearly and appealingly presented.